THE RESTLANDS

Sara Rust

THE RESTLANDS

ISBN 978-0-692-04073-7

Library of Congress Control Number: 2018912142

Photos courtesy of unsplash.com

To order more books or to learn more about the author, please visit the author's website: www.saramrust.com

Published by Porch & Story Creative Studios, Montgomery, TX

Printed in the USA

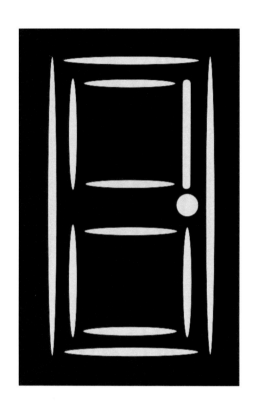

It's open.

Trail Guide

Acknowledgements

To my parents. You have sacrificed more than I'll know for me to chase after what is in my heart. Thank you for believing in me and loving me well. One of these days, when this all pays off, I will take you to Italy and treat you to gelato.

To my Pathway family. I had only just found you when I first started writing this story. You were a perfectly timed gift in my life. Thank you for celebrating me, encouraging me, praying for me, holding me when I could not stop the tears, fixing my car, calling out my voice, and believing I could do whatever God put in my heart. I feel honored to call you family.

A letter to my book on its birthday.

Hey, Little One.

It's time. Time to take a deep breath, straighten out your new clothes, and walk out into the world.

I am so proud of you. You are special, you know that? When we first met, I wasn't sure who you were. I was in a bad spot, you remember. I needed hope, and light, and to believe that life would be beautiful again. And then you showed up. Small. Unassuming. And moment by breathtaking moment, you awakened life in me again.

I could keep you all to myself. I wouldn't mind a bit. But I think you are much bigger than you know, Little One. I want you to go and share your story, share your moments, share your ways. The way you talk about love has changed me. And even if there is one - just one other who hears your tale and who sees for the first time that Love has been chasing them down, what a wonder that would be.

So, off you go, my brave story. There is nothing I need from you. Our adventure was more than satisfying. Be you. Be love. Be free.

Have a wonderful journey.

The Rest Stop

My journey to the Restlands began on a highway. Careening through forest-lined mountainsides, the road was accompanied on one side by an eager river. Now, before you picture this scene as me on the open road, rockin' it like a truck commercial, you should probably know that this particular highway was bumper to bumper for miles. In fact, I don't recall a time when I didn't see a steady stream of vehicles. Luckily, the cars moved together as if perched on a giant conveyor belt, and never slowed down.

Happy faces. Happy cars. Everyone driving with expectation and intention and wonder. Cause that's what you do on the Highway of Dreams and Ambition. I loved this road. What better place to be than surrounded by dreamers, all gleefully wondering *are we there yet?* The GPS was our beloved sidekick counting down the mileage until we had at last – *arrived.*

So when my turn signal inadvertently went on, there were a few choice words that went through my mind.

What is going on? Um. Why are we getting off here? We were getting closer - this is a waste of -

The sign on the off ramp was simple: Rest Area.

Rest area?! Are you kidding me? We don't have time for -

And as if on cue, the radio turned on and crooned *Jesus take the wheel.*

The humor of heaven, ladies and gentleman. I knew exactly who

was behind this unplanned detour. My car pulled into a parking spot and there He was, standing with a warm smile, dressed like He just stepped out of a trendy outdoor outfitters.

Now, it's hard to be irritated at Papa, He is, after all, love incarnate. But I will bashfully admit – I was miffed. The constant zipping of cars behind me punctuated in rhythmic fashion how I was now off schedule.

"Hey, Kiddo," He hugged me after I closed the car door.

"Papa." I melted, His affection always the perfect remedy for my bad attitude.

He motioned to the view, "What do you think?"

I nodded and smiled, "Pretty amazing, actually, Papa." I'd been enjoying the view on my long drive, but it's interesting how animated the trees and river looked now that I was standing still.

"I've got something for you," He winked and stepped aside revealing a pristine hiker's pack, filled and ready, and a pair of boots.

"Wow," I knelt down to inspect my new gift as my heart surprisingly – sank. I looked over my shoulder at the highway as I realized this was not a quick stop. *Everything's passing me by.* I felt his hand on my shoulder.

"You won't find what you are looking for there," He said gently, "What you are looking for is here – in the Restlands."

"The Restlands?"

He knelt down and handed me a leather-bound journal, "to write about our journey."

"Journey?" I couldn't stop looking back at the road. It was strangely magnetic in this moment. Then He asked *that* question. The question that He had been asking before I even got out of the car. The question I'd heard a million times, whispering in my mind as I plastered a smile on my face and kept driving.

"How's that road treating your heart, Scribe?"

There it was. He already knew the answer, of course. But He never asks these questions for Himself. He already knew I was wearing down. I'd been working hard to pursue my dreams, to fund my dreams, to become more fully who I was created to be. And He saw me – ripping at my seams of sanity and joy. He saw my heart begin to fall out of me like an old transmission. Pushing, pushing to make everyone happy, to make me happy, and failing often on both accounts. And He knew I would have pushed through until I completely fell apart. The road had been rough on my heart. I didn't want to admit it or give up all I'd worked for.

But in His kindness, He turned on my blinker.

I hadn't said a word. My tears were loud enough. He brushed them away while offering the kindest smile. "I've seen, Scribe. I've seen what you can do working hard. I am a proud Papa – always." He rose slowly and offered His hand to help me up, "Let's watch what I can do when you *rest*."

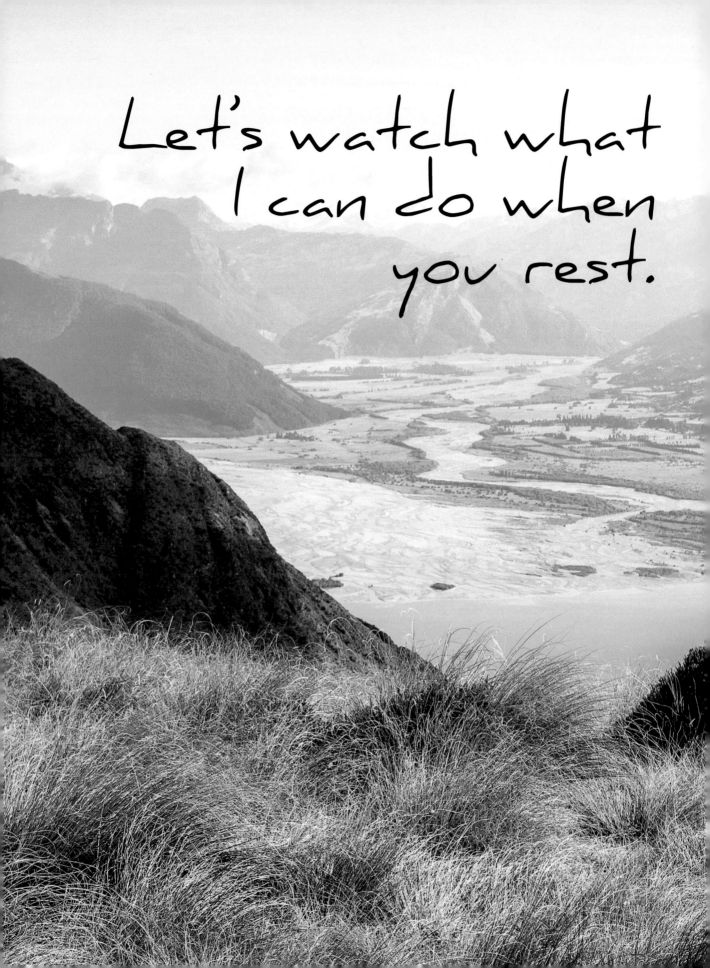

-Papa

2

No Strings Attached

It took about a mile to discover two indisputable facts. Papa loved to whistle and the backpack was killing me. *What did He put in this thing?*

I didn't think much of the songs he was chortling until I heard the birds join in. *Oh, man. This was awesome.* It was like some storybook fairytale. Melodies, trees, and sunbeams. Classic. I was keeping my eyes peeled for Sleeping Beauty or Bambi to scamper through, when the music suddenly stopped – and Papa let out the loudest laugh.

I paused behind him on the trail and watched as he swayed back and forth, holding his belly. Between chuckles He'd try and speak, "Did you hear that one, Scribe? Oh, they are on a roll today!"

"Wait. Are you – are you bantering with the birds, Papa?"

He turned around to face me, wiping a tear, "So funny."

I stood studying Him and the trees wondering what the punch line was and also if I could put the pack down. *Did I mention it was killing me?* I think He caught sight of my pained smile as He continued to wipe tears from His cheeks.

"Oh, Scribe, let me get that for you."

"Really?"

He nodded helping me take the pack off and placing it on His back, "Yes, of course. I'm always happy to carry your stuff." He winked. "Just as long as you don't mind carrying mine."

"But Papa you don't have any stuff," I laughed.

He smiled turning back on the trail.

His burden is light. I thought, or maybe He said it. It was hard to tell sometimes. We continued down the trail and admittedly, it was so much easier trekking without the pack. As my back stretched out, I felt freer to appreciate the beauty of the trail. The Restlands felt familiar, the aspen and pine reminding me of childhood hikes in Colorado. But at the same time there was this sense that something out of the ordinary could happen at any moment, like finding an Ewok village or a group of elves showing up to offer me cookies. I might have been hungry.

Papa continued to waltz down the trail at a pretty pace, and even without the pack I struggled to keep up.

"Papa, can you wait up?"

He turned and walked back to me posthaste. "No problem, Kiddo. How about you set the pace?"

"Okay," I breathed heavily, "It's just – I mean it feels easier not carrying all my stuff, thank you – but I feel like something is pulling on me. It's weird."

"Hmm." Papa looked behind me, "Could be *those.*"

I turned around to find several strings attached to me as if I was tied to something at the trailhead.

"What in the world?" I reached around to examine them closer. Tiny strings – with words written all over them. My words. My thoughts. The ones I'd been mulling in my mind since the beginning of the trail. I took one in my hand and read the words on the string for several feet. Most of the sentences began with, *If I would have…* or *I should have…*

Papa drew near to me, but said nothing.

I looked up at Him teary-eyed, "These are my thoughts, Papa. These are all the things I wish I would have done – or not done."

"So you could have stayed on the road?" He put his arm around me.

I nodded. "Cause I failed, right? I mean that's why I'm here. *Cause I failed.* I couldn't hack it – like everyone else." My tears flooded his shirt.

He squeezed me and kissed my forehead, "You didn't fail me, Kiddo. The Restlands is not a punishment – it's a gift. I'm so thankful you are here."

I turned to pick up the strings again, "Sorry I'm such a mess, Papa."

His eyes caught mine, even as I tried to avoid them, and He smiled, "Actually, you're perfect." He let the words hang in the air as He looked at me waiting for them to sink into my heart.

I nodded, hopeful they would.

"Now. Shall we untie these? Seems very hard to explore The Restlands with all this – *regret.*" Papa had this charming way of making things that felt overwhelming sound like a piece of cake.

"I think I'd like that."

He didn't miss a beat, and went right to work helping untie all the strings, whistling all the while. When we finished, I shook my hands and stretched my back.

"So proud of you, my Scribe," He hugged me.

I took a deep breath, "Thanks, Papa."

"Shall we?" He picked up the pack and pointed down the trail and then we began to walk, "Hey, wanna hear a good joke, Scribe? I just heard the best one."

I grinned up at the trees and rolled my eyes in amusement, "Yeah, Papa. I'd love it."

The Restlands

is not a

punishment -

it's a gift.

- Papa

3

Comparing Lists

As we sat by the fire, I watched Him. Creator of the cosmos, whittling a stick. Equal parts awe and simplicity, grandeur and comfort. Choosing now to sit with me. And all I could think about, holding my open journal, was how many more important things He could be doing right now.

That's when He paused, looked up and softly offered, "Why would I want to be anywhere else?" He raised an eyebrow and added, "And who's to say I'm not?"

We'd been on the trail for a few days by then. I tried on several occasions to get intel from Papa – namely, *where* we were actually going. True, we were exploring the Restlands, but even explorers have a destination, right? Every time I asked if we were getting closer, Papa would look me in the eye, pause, and simply respond, "Could be." *Could be*? Shouldn't He know? If mystery were the currency of the Restlands, this land was flowing with milk and honey.

Conversations with Papa were like a song. He knew when to crescendo and when to rest. He listened happily to my musings on life, pointed out different beauties on the trail, and then left me to the sounds of nature and my own thoughts. It was effortless and kind. Even the silences felt safe. I didn't ask a lot of questions the first few days, to be honest. I could have asked Him about the creation of all things or dinosaurs or what Mary and

Joseph were like as parents. But I didn't. Being with Him was more satisfying than knowing all the answers. So I let questions rise as they desired.

Each night Papa would set up a hammock for me amongst the trees and prepare a meal around the fire. I would pull out my journal, write about the day, draw silly pictures – and He would whittle. Ever the carpenter. I would watch Him whittle for a while, and then He would watch me write. I knew He was watching. It sounds strange, but I could feel Him smiling while He did.

"Papa?" I looked up from my journal, noting His grin.

"Yes, Scribe?"

"This place – this Restlands. It's supposed to help me rest, right?"

"That would be a very happy outcome, I would think, don't you?"

"Yes, I mean after life on the road. It would be very nice to rest. It's just that…" I stretched my sore leg, "it's kind of a lot of work."

He nodded, "What did you think rest was?"

"Less mileage. More hammock," I smiled.

He laughed, "I understand."

"I guess. I don't really know where you're taking me – I'm sure it's going to be great, can't wait to see it – *for real*. I'm just not feeling super rested. Just being honest. But with all this trail time, I've been doing some soul searching, and I've sort of made a list."

"A list?" He leaned forward, amused.

"Yeah. Uh. A list of things I think if we took care of – then I could rest." I sat up straight, ready to make my proposal.

"Oh, great. Me too."

"You have a list too?"

"Sure do," He put his wood down and folded His hands ready to listen, "But you first, what's on your list?"

I slowly handed Him my journal.

He rested his chin in his hand and began to read the list, then turn a page of the journal. Then another page. And then another. "Wow, this is *quite* a list, Scribe. You know you've got a few things down here more than once."

"Yeah, I just figure we should *really* address those items. Get 'em done real good, you know, Papa? Cause then I can really enter in – and enjoy all the resting. Get that Hebrews 4 rockin' and rollin' in my life, right?"

His mouth was open, but the corners were turned up. I think this was entertaining for Him.

"Good list, Scribe. I can understand why you want all of those things taken care of in your life – how it speaks of rest to you. My list is a bit shorter, would you be interested in hearing it? I didn't write it down, hope that's okay." He handed my journal back to me.

"Oh, yes. Of course, Papa. A shorter list sounds amazing. Let me write this down." I waited with pencil in hand.

He spoke. I wrote. And in a moment it was done. Papa's To-Do list in the Restlands:

> Know Him.
>
> Know me.
>
> Everything else was just details.

I crept into my hammock thinking of Papa's list and took a deep breath. *What had I signed up for?* Papa hummed a tune by the fire, whittling away as slumber tucked me in to another day's end in the Restlands.

- directions for life
- finances
- clean out email
- finances
- get super healthy
- family stuff
- marriage? kids?
are we tabling that?
- finances
- go through old
boxes
- make sure I'm not
crazy

Papa's List
1. Know Me
2. Know You
3. Details

4

Building the Tree House

Know Him. Know Me. Everything else was just details. I'd been thinking of Papa's list as we descended through the trees on the trail. As crazy as it may sound, despite His list being a good five or so pages shorter than mine, I wasn't convinced it was entirely easier. *How do I know Him? How do I know if I know Him enough? How do I know me? Did I really know me at all?* My thoughts swirled and my eyes began to cross just as Papa's voice chimed in, "Don't think too hard, Scribe. It's not good for the heart."

I'd heard that before somewhere.

He stopped ahead, turned and smiled. We had come to a clearing, the entrance to a valley, and Papa stood as if He was waiting to open the doors to a great hall. We'd been hiking in the trees for days, but now the blue skies above stretched out wide and the sound of a stream bid us enter into flat lands. Wildflowers sprinkled the fields like confetti while the birds traced the mountainsides. It was quite a postcard.

Even down to the enchanting giant oak tree that sat right in the middle of the scene. The one the stream flowed straight underneath. The one you'd never forget if you'd ever seen it. *Which I had*. Which is why I was freaking out at this moment.

"What in the world? I've been here, Papa."

"I remember." He took a stick and threw it into the water to watch it float under the tree.

Of course He remembers. We'd been here a dozen times. This is where I sat and wrote some very treasured Invitations. Right up there in that –

"Wait, Papa. Where is it? Where's the tree house?" I looked up all around the top of the tree, but there was no sign of it. The one that held the library and the desk. The one where I would write, and He would sit, and we would talk for hours.

"I love that place," He said placing the backpack on the ground. He opened the pack and pulled out a tool belt, "Let's build it."

"Let's – *what*?" Clearly I was insane. "Build the tree house that was *already* built – the one that sat happily atop that tree for years, and is now gone?!"

Papa laughed a little, "Yeah. That one." He handed me a hammer.

"Is this for my head?" I paced in a circle for a good thirty seconds talking to myself about wormholes and time travel, which Papa only found more amusing.

He finally reached out His arm to pause my rotations, "Scribe."

I nodded.

"Time is my playground. Don't think too hard, it's not good for the heart. Let's build."

By nightfall we had the ladder and the landing finished. Papa hung my hammock and a lantern from the branches in what would become the library – or what once was the library? I was still unsure about this time ripple of sorts.

"Thanks for all your help today, Scribe."

"Of course." I sat swinging in my hammock looking at the beginnings of the treehouse. I imagined the bookshelves and the balcony and the wingback chair where Papa would always sit when we'd talk. I looked at Papa now, stretched out on the landing with his arms behind His head. "I didn't know I was here when the treehouse was built."

He grinned still looking at the stars above, "And yet, here you are."

And yet, here I was. Swinging in certainty that I knew what would be. I knew where the bags of jacks would sit one day, and the music box, and the baseball glove. And there was Papa, laid out on the floorboards rocking his foot back and forth, also knowing everything that would be.

I crept out of my hammock and joined Him on the floor, lacing my fingers behind my head and turning to study His face. "Was it finished before it began?"

He caught a leaf as it fell from the branch above. I'm sure He knew at this point I wasn't talking about the tree house. I was searching for an answer. I was trying to unpack a riddle. What was the purpose of building the tree house today? What did this have to do with rest – or knowing Him – or knowing me?

"Yes," He caught another leaf falling from the branch, "In the beginning, it was finished." Papa's words pervaded the half-built room like a heavy fog. "When you know everything's done – you can rest."

I took a deep breath and looked up, that's when I watched the rafters appear out of thin air, followed by the bookshelves, and the railing on the balcony. Papa's chair had arrived and the ballet slippers were right where I left them by the desk. And suddenly, as if awakening from a dream, the tree house was finished.

"Well done, Scribe." He sat up and scanned the shelves picking out a book and placing it on my desk, which had also kindly appeared. He tapped the book inviting me to read.

I rose, placing my hands on the desk, looking closely at the wood to see if I could find familiar grooves from my favorite pen. I breathed deeply at their happy appearance and recalled a flurry of moments writing stories in this very place. I noticed the book He chose and grinned. *"The Book Maker?"* One of my favorites. I turned to the first page and began to read.

We exchanged bedtime tales through the early morning, kept company by the light from the fireplace, while the Restlands waited for our next move.

5

The Ugly Cry

I traced the lines of words in my journal until they were nearly black. We were back on the trail, but the tree house remained a playful puzzle in my mind.

I knew better than to wrestle to understand it all. Instead I would take what I could, like drinking water from the sky as it rained. A few drops of peace knowing He was always with me. A few drops of comfort knowing He knew the journey before I started walking it. A few drops of wonder that I walked in freedom in this mystery.

We had followed the stream from the tree house and found a place to rest sitting on some large rocks. Papa sat quietly, whittling away, and occasionally looked up to smile at the scenery. He was never in a rush. Or at least, He never seemed to have a desire to rush me. I could stop or sit anytime, without saying a word – and Papa would follow suit. No questions. No words. I think He knew when I needed to be still for a few moments.

And all it took was a few moments. I tried blinking my eyes and shaking my head, but the tears paid no attention as they streamed in gentle fashion down my cheeks. Papa was quick to catch my journal before it fell into the stream and draw to my side, wrapping me in His arms. He held me tight as I began to shake.

"There it is," He said, "You've been holding onto that a long time."

The drops were unrelenting with no decorum. Poor Papa was covered in tears and snot, as I sobbed, my eyes inadequate to release all the grief inside.

He rocked me for hours. At least it felt like hours. As my body grew weary, I reached up to feel the top of my head. Papa's tears had soaked my hair.

Jesus wept, I thought. He wept with me. I looked up at Him, wiping my own eyes so I could clearly see His. This One so great and mighty was unapologetically tear-stained. This left me speechless as I studied Him. Was it strange that He looked stronger to me now? My hand found His cheek before I was aware, and I brushed His tears while whispering, "Blessed are those who mourn, for they will be comforted."

He kissed my forehead and returned my journal. "How do you feel, Scribe?"

"Better. I think." I examined my shirt, but realized Papa's got the brunt of the damage, "Oh, Papa, I'm so sorry." I tried to clean it off, but He reassured me it was no bother. "I'm not sure what I was even crying about. It just kind of came over me and I couldn't stop."

"There's only so many *I'm fine's* the heart can take before it reveals itself."

I instinctively put my hand on my heart, "I just didn't think there was time for such things on the road. Just stay positive and it'll all work out, you know? Hope rises. Love wins. No one wants to listen to the blues when they're driving."

"When there is loss, there is grief. And it's okay to grieve   to let the sadness take its course, Scribe, and find its way out of your heart. For when it remains, when you try to silence it with jingles of *look on the bright side* and *be thankful for what you do have*, the sadness is not appeased, only trapped by platitudes. Sometimes the bravest thing you can do is cry. Let the sadness go. And welcome the joys when you finish drying your eyes." He took my hand, "Because hope *does* rise. Love *does* win. This is not how the story ends." Papa wiped fresh tears from His cheeks. "Oh, Joy!" He got up looked all around, "Oh, she should be around here somewhere. You're going to *love* her."

"Love *her*?" It was like she was some fellow hiker we would meet on the trail.

"Yep. She's hard not to love." Papa held his hand out and helped me up.

I stood in the middle of the stream watching it bend over the edge of the small cliff edge. I could hear the anthem of the waterfall below and thought how remarkable the strength of water is when it falls, chiseling rock as it flows, and I wondered if my tears had the same power – to chisel the hardest parts of my heart and mind into something beautiful. Something free. Something truly – at rest.

Sometimes
the bravest
thing you can
do is cry.
-Papa

6

Joy Unleashed

Papa was a little ways ahead on the trail, whistling as usual, when I heard rustling in the bush behind me. Not the scurry of a wily squirrel or bird in the brush. It was something – *bigger*.

"Papa," I whispered hoping He would stop. I turned slowly to investigate. The bush was too small to hide a grizzly or a wolf. But it might be a snake – or an angry miniature moose – or a baby bear set as a trap by mama bear to lure me in. I pictured several intense scenarios of how the creature in the bush was going to finish me off when I heard Papa beside me with a low voice.

"What is it, Scribe?"

"Something's in that bush." I tiptoed behind Him and peered around his shoulder.

He laughed, "I don't think you want to hide from her."

Hide from her? I stepped out just far enough from Papa to see her eyes locked on me as she made her ferocious departure from the bush, running at me like a bull in Pamplona. Small, but mighty, she knocked me over, heading straight for my face. I couldn't see anything through the fluff and kisses, but could hear Papa dropping to His knees, laughing. About the time I could have succumbed to death-by-affection, He called her.

"Come here, Joy! Come here, girl!" He patted the ground.

Joy paused, and gave me one more lick for good measure before racing over to Papa. She ran in little circles around Him and then froze, assuming the position for a belly rub. This gave me enough time to wipe my face repeatedly with my sleeves and sit up. "Joy's a puppy?"

He scratched her behind the ears, "Such a good girl. We've been wondering where you were, Joy." She flipped over and sat with her tongue out.

I moved my feet in an attempt to get up and she turned to me and pranced over. I braced for impact, but Joy sat quietly in front of me this time, head cocked to the side as she looked me over. Noticing the silver bell that hung from her blue collar, I reached my hand out slowly to check for tags, "Who does she belong to?"

Papa rose brushing the dirt off his pants, "Everyone."

"Everyone? But who takes care of her? Where does she live?"

"Anyone can take care of her, she likes to roam around out here." He twirled his hand over Joy's head until she danced around on her back two feet, "Friendly little thing, isn't she?"

I patted my face, still wet, "She's so cute, Papa. Can we keep her?"

"I'm quite sure there's nothing that would make her happier, Scribe."

I twirled my hand above Joy's head as I attempted to make her dance. But she would have none of it and instead chose to run like a crazy dog up and down the trail until her enthusiasm outran her legs and she tumbled over. "Is she okay?" I reached down to pick her up.

"She's fine. Wildly unpredictable at times, but she'll come when you call her."

"Can we teach her some tricks?" I stroked her head as she nuzzled into my arms.

"You can't train Joy, Scribe," He patted her head, then turned to start on the trail again, "but you can befriend her."

It's hard to compare the cute factor when it comes to puppies, but Joy was the most adorable one I'd seen to date. I leaned my head down close to her ear and whispered, "Be my friend, Joy."

Papa, now a good ways down on the trail shouted, "She likes you, Scribe. She likes you a lot. You may have a hard time getting rid of her."

I squeezed her close and added, "That's okay with me, Joy." And with that, she leapt from my arms and chased Papa like a bullet down the trail.

Our tribe of two became a tribe of three and my heart was happy at our growing band of explorers. Meeting Joy was a happy day on the trail.

But it was also the first day I heard the footsteps behind us.

Joy is the friend to befriend in the Restlands. Such a loyal little thing. Though it seems she believes she is much bigger than she is. Maybe she is much bigger than she is. Maybe I could be too. Bigger. Braver. More like Joy. Such a funny, wild pup. Joy pursues. She chases you down. I can not own her, but she can not help but own me.

I can't help but think that she was always meant to feel at home with me – and I with her.

7

The Wardrobe

You hear a lot of things in the Restlands. Birds banter with acute comic timing (according to Papa). Leaves catch the simplest breeze to start a tune. Waterfalls stream a happy percussion. It's all very National Geographic. But hearing footsteps behind you was an oddity.

So much so, that I initially ignored them. *Must be a squirrel scampering across the trail or the bending of branches in the wind.* I didn't always hear them. But on this day I knew they had to be real, because they sounded so close. And I was sure I heard *breathing*.

Joy was already on her hundredth dash back and forth between Papa and I, when I barreled down the trail to catch up to Him. "Uh, Papa," I sputtered, catching my breath, "I think someone's behind us."
He turned. And I turned, slowly. But there was no one there. Just Joy, running in circles and hoping on lizards.

"Are there others out here, Papa?" We hadn't seen anyone, but surely – it was such a big place, there were others out exploring.

"Why wouldn't there be?" Papa squinted looking out into the woods, then looked down at me. "We could be close."

Close? To where we were going? Were we meeting someone? Why was He staring at me?

"Could be very close. Come on, Scribe." He returned to saunter down the trail.

"Wait, what?" I hesitated to turn around, trying to keep my eyes on the mystery. "Wait up!" I shuffled quickly to catch up to Him, looking behind me every few moments just to make sure until I bumped right into Papa.

"Woah, Kiddo. Slow down and breathe. Look." He grabbed the straps of the backpack and nodded ahead.

I peeked around Papa. *Oh, my Clive Staples. It couldn't be.* The trail opened to a small clearing amongst the trees, and right at its center stood a large wooden wardrobe. I paused long enough to notice Joy rubbing her back while circling around the wardrobe's legs. Seconds later, I may or may not have been hugging the furniture and mumbling sweet nothings to the land of Narnia.

"She's a beaut, huh, Scribe?" Papa said giving the wardrobe a good pat on its side.

"Oh my gosh, Papa. Can we go inside? This place is awesome. I *love* rest!"

He laughed, "Yes, you can go inside. But I'm going to wait right here. Take your time though – and take whatever you'd like." He turned the handle to open the door.

"Take whatever I like?" I blinked as the wardrobe doors opened. There were no fur coats. No woods. No lamppost. Just a very elegant and embarrassingly large dressing room with rich lighting and gobs of clothing hung and folded with precision all around. I carefully stepped inside as the doors closed and wondered why we had stopped for a shopping spree in the Restlands.

My fingers danced over silk blouses and studied ornate, embroidered dresses. On one of the walls was a shelf with heels in every color, a rung full of scarves, and several drawers sparkling with jewelry. It was obviously time to have a Pretty Woman moment. I rolled up my sleeves and bounced my knees like a runner taking her mark. In a whirl, I was off – dashing around the dressing room trying on every possible item.

Sundresses were my favorite for a good twenty minutes before I found the evening gowns. There was a beautiful, long black number complete with gloves – very Audrey Hepburn – that I may have spent some time in while practicing an Oscar acceptance speech in front of the mirror. *But one would, wouldn't they?*

There was a familiarity to all the clothes and as I reached for a pink cashmere sweater, I discovered why. The clothes had no tags. Instead, sewn inside each one was a piece of cream cloth with someone's name printed on it. Names of people I knew. Names of people I admired. I began picking the clothing off the floor and reading the names. This one had the name of a woman who ran an orphanage. Another had the name of an incredible educator. Or a mom I thought was amazing. Or a missionary. Or an entrepreneur. Or a writer. Or a friend.

I picked up a blouse with the name of a favorite singer and tried it on. I stood looking at myself in the mirror. I looked uncomfortable, though the blouse was so beautiful. My mind wrestled to convince me to take it – make it my own – because I loved the one who wore it. I stared around the room, piles of admiration all across the floor. *How many times have I tried to put on someone else's outfit? Someone else's calling? Someone else's dream? So desperate to make it my own. So enamored by the stories of others, I hadn't noticed I had yet to find my own.*

Know me, He said.

I scanned the dressing room and smiled as I stooped to pick up a pair of Chacos that had been covered in the mess of heels. I spotted a pair of jeans, a white shirt, a plaid button down, and the piece-de-resistance – a gray hoodie. After careful inspection I realized none of these items had names on them and quickly put them on. The woman in the mirror took a deep breath. She looked happier. She wore a fresh story. One that could be her own. I grabbed a baseball cap off a nearby hook as I went to open the doors and tucked it in my back pocket.

"That's all your taking?" Papa asked, eyebrows raised.

"I think it's all I need."

Joy licked my exposed toes and rolled over to ask for a tummy rub.

"We may be very close indeed." Papa winked, then paused to look behind us, where I'd heard the footsteps. "We've got some hiking to do." Papa whistled for Joy to join Him as he turned back on the trail. I scurried to catch up.

8

The All-Nighter

Papa made camp as usual. He hung my hammock, made a fire, cooked our food and began to whittle. Joy was curled up by my feet, snoring. All the lizard chasing had taken its toll. I watched Papa in the firelight, carefully crafting His wood for hours. I wondered if he had looked as intent fashioning Canis Majoris. Then I wondered what He looked like when He formed me. The thought frightened me at first as I imagined some cosmic conveyor belt where mankind passed before Him and He assembled us like little Lego characters.

"Scribe?" He interrupted.

"Yes," I blinked looking up at Him, forgetting He could hear my inner dialogue.

"I'm not Geppetto."

"Geppetto, Papa?"

"You are not the product of a childless man, a mere toy come to life to appease me. I did not whittle you out of wood Scribe, I whittled you out of Me." Then He winked, "We're family. And I'm sorry, there's nothing you can do about it."

I rose to hug Him goodnight, but somehow got stuck sitting next to Him, leaning with my head on His shoulder. The flames bopped and swayed, dancing with the wind. He kissed my head as I sighed.

"If everyone who had ever lived wrote all they'd ever seen you do and all they'd ever heard you say, I don't imagine it would come very close to explaining how good you are. The page strains to contain you, Papa. I think I have run out of words." I stroked the journal in my lap.

He didn't respond, but in the quiet of my mind I heard Him, *In the beginning was the Word, and the Word was with God, and the Word was God. So the Word became human and made His home among us.*

"You came for us."

His knife cut deep into the wood as He carved, "There was a bit of confusion about who I am."

And then I heard Him again, *I am the visible image of the invisible God. I perfectly express His character. I am the exact representation, the perfect imprint of the essence of God.*

I sat up and pulled away from Papa, His words fought my heart. I wondered if it was even right for me to be so near to Him – God incarnate. His next words cut deep, like His knife was whittling my heart.

"Who do you say I am, Scribe?"

I sat squirming and I'm sure He could tell. It felt like a test and I wondered if I'd be kicked out of the Restlands if I didn't answer correctly. *He was my Father, and friend. But also my safety and provider. He was God but also man, but also holy and kind. He was relatable and revered. He was my savior and redeemer and all the other churchy terms I'd learned over my life. The answer should be simple, right? It usually is with Him.* There were a million words and no words at the same time. But somehow in the mess of them all, out it came.

"You are my home and my great adventure."

He carefully put down His knife and wood and turned to offer both of His hands, "Then, you need never draw away, Scribe."

I gently placed my hands in His and caught for the first time the sight of scars under the cuffs of his plaid shirt. The light from the fire only gave hints of what was truly there. He held my hands tighter as they began to tremble, sprinkled by the tears from my eyes. The grief hit me like a hammer, "I'm so sorry," I whispered.

He pressed His forehead against mine. "I know."

I closed my eyes wanting to hide from the answer of the question I was about to ask, "Papa, who do you say we are?" I had a choice selection of responses I thought fitting for Him to use: monsters, ungrateful, blind, hateful, hurtful, lost. But He decided to go a different direction. If words could be quilted into sheets of comfort, His were a perfect pattern of peace, wonder, and hope.

"You are my home and my great adventure."

It was about this time that Joy rolled over and stretched from her slumber. She smacked her lips and noticed our small pow-wow, and without prompting sprung to her feet, pranced over and jumped right into my lap where she proceeded to lick the tears off my cheeks.

"Joy!" I laughed, trying to push her down so I could breathe.

Papa picked her up and she nuzzled in His arms, "Such a good, girl, Joy."

Sunlight tip-toed into camp as the fire dimmed and the birds began to stir. We'd been up all night.

"Why don't you rest a little while I make some breakfast, Scribe? I think today's going to be a big day."

And He was right.

This was the day we met the one who was following us.

You are my great

home and my
adventure.
-Papa

9

The Wrestling Match

We must have made it.

"Quite a scene, isn't it Scribe?" Papa laid the pack down as He watched the sun set. The mountains cradled the great lake and rocked it softly as the day drew to a close.

"Yes. It's perfect, Papa." I admired dusk in the Restlands while looking around intently for – for something. If this is where the trail ended, shouldn't there be something, well, *climatic*? A secret door? A treasure chest? A place to throw an evil ring to save Middle Earth? I wasn't asking for much.

Papa laughed. "You crack me up, Kid."

"Sorry, I just thought since the trail has come to an end," I motioned to the water, "that this is where it would happen."

"What would happen?"

"Um. I don't know. Whatever big thing it is that has to happen for me to understand rest."

"I see." He looked at me curiously as He skipped a stone across the lake. "Perhaps rest is about more than arriving."

His words played in my mind, so simple at first. How often had I relegated rest to a stop on the road? I supposed it would be there waiting for me once I finally – got married or had children or paid off debt or wrote that book or was in perfect health or – whatever. I thought these were the precursors to rest, and, in turn, the antidotes to restlessness. Highway rule 101. You can rest when you get there. But rest was turning out to be far greater than a stop on the road – maybe it had nothing to do with arriving or achieving.

"It's not something I can chase, is it, Papa?"

He shook His head, "How can you chase something that's been following you all your life?"

I held my arms and took a deep breath.

"I'm going to go gather some wood for the fire. Do you want to come with me?"

"I think I'll stay here, Papa." I kicked the dirt lightly with my feet.

Papa nodded and smiled, then ambled down the beach a ways, whistling with Joy in pursuit. About the time I could no longer hear His song or His steps – I heard hers.

But this time, the one who had been following us did not step quietly. Her feet pounded the ground like a wild horse. Before I could turn to see her, she tackled me to the ground.

"Papa!" I screamed before my face hit the dirt. I kicked and pushed, trying to release her grip around my shoulders, "Papa, help me!"

"I am."

Did *she* say that? Was that in my head? The dimming light made identifying her a challenged as we tumbled on the beach. "Let go of me!" I yelled.

She didn't respond and continued to try and pin me down. I braced myself as we spun again and then tried to push with hand and foot to stand up. Her hair hid her face amidst the tousle. I flipped her to the ground and held her wrists. "Who are you?" I wailed as she heaved forward and knocked me over.

My shoulder landed on a jagged rock, "Stop!" At once, she backed off. I reached for my shoulder with my other hand and felt blood. *What is this madness?* I sat up slowly trying to get a better look at my injury. Bruised and battered for sure, but I could move it a little. I looked up at the wild one and held one hand out hoping she would keep her distance, "What is going on? Who are you?"

She brushed her hands on her jeans, and moved the hair from in front of her face.

How could this be? I moved back, shuffling my feet in the dirt.

She picked up her hat from the ground, adjusted her hoodie, and placed it on her head. Her Chacos were every bit as dirty as mine.

"Who are you?" I blinked.

"I didn't think I'd need an introduction."

"But – what? How?" I had no idea what to say. How do you respond to an opponent when she turns out to be – *you*? I cradled my shoulder, "I don't understand."

She held out her hands, reassuring me no harm, and sat down on a large rock.

I shook my head like an etch-a-sketch, trying to reset everything. *Close your eyes. It's all a dream.*

"It's not a dream," she said.

"How is this possible? How did I just have a wrestling match with myself?"

"I didn't come to fight you." She looked serious.

I looked at my shoulder and winced, "What?"

"You wouldn't let me go."

"*I* wouldn't let *you* go?"

"You've been fighting me for a while."

"I've been fighting *you*?!" I would have gotten up then and stormed out of the room, except there was no room and I was unsure where to storm off to, "Why would I be fighting *you?*"

"Because love feels like hell when you can't receive it."

I looked at her blankly. I examined the dirt, the tree branches, the lapping water trying to make sense of this moment. "You tackled me to love me?"

"No, I never tackled you. But you have perceived my presence as a wrestling match."

"I've been wrestling with myself?"

"For a while now."

"About what?" I sat up on my knees.

She leaned forward, "Who are you?"

Was this a trick question? "I'm Scribe."

"No. Who are you?"

"I told you. My name is Scribe." I annunciated, hoping it would help.

"No." She folded her hands, "Scribe is what you do. I asked you who you are."

I bit my lip. *Who was I without my trail name? What was I apart from what I could do, what I could offer, how I could serve?*

This was the great wrestling, to rest in the value that was simply being me. Nothing added. Nothing required. Always enough.

"Be gentle with yourself, Sara."

My name. The sound of it cascaded over me, like a waterfall rinsing away the weight of every obligation I'd put on myself.

The birds chirped as the last light dimmed and the wild one laughed. *Wait a minute. She was laughing at the birds just like Papa.* I leaned forward and watched her smile as I heard deep inside, *I am you when rest, at last, settles in. Christ in you, the hope of glory.*

Then a branch snapped and I looked up to see Papa carrying a load of kindling to the campsite, still whistling. Joy was proudly carrying a stick of her own. I turned to look at the wild one. But she was gone.

"I bet you must be hungry. I'll be quick."

"A little. Here, let me help you, Papa." I got up carefully and patted my shoulder – but there was no wound. No blood. No scratch. No scar. I bent down to pick up a large piece of wood though, and winced at the pain.

"Are you okay, Sara?"

My name. He said my name. "My shoulder's a little sore, Papa."

"It could use a little rest I'm sure," He looked up at me and smiled. I left the fire building to Papa and soon sat beside Him devouring the warm dinner, "Do we head back tomorrow, Papa?

"Head back?"

"Why sure, cause there's no more trail." I nodded to the lake. He grinned, "Who says there's no more trail?" And He too nodded towards the lake.

10

The Impossible Task

Joy came to me in the morning. I woke to her licking my face. This had become her ritual, the rising sun her cue to kiss me awake. And I would always respond by tickling her belly until her leg shook and her little tongue rolled out of her mouth. When she couldn't take anymore, she'd run up and down the length of the hammock until we'd tumble out onto the ground – well, at least I would. Joy would always make this graceful leap towards the campfire. I can still see her cheeky little grin turning to watch me fall onto the ground. It repeats in slow motion in my mind when I need a laugh.

Papa was serving breakfast as I made my way to a happy log next to the fire. Joy, ever the morning pup, pranced near the water and proceeded to do a series of stretches, jumps, and sprints.

"How's the shoulder?" Papa asked handing me a steaming plate.

"A little sore, to be honest. Will it always be sore?"

"Could be." He smiled, stirring some fresh coffee.

The Restlands was full of *could bes*, that's for sure. We talked for a while that morning. I asked Him all kinds of crazy questions about theology and life. Three of which made Him spit out His coffee. What I loved the most about asking Papa questions was He never seemed to think they were stupid. There was no condescension, no *how could you ask that*, *the answer is so obvious*, no *you should know that by now*. Every question was fair game with

Him. His eyes would light up and He'd lean in with His fingers trilling the sides of His coffee mug with the enthusiasm of a Dad teaching his kid about the family business. Even with all the mystery of the Restlands, truth remained a topic of great passion for Papa. I think He could have sat there all day shooting the breeze, but when I asked Him where we were headed next, He jumped into action packing up the camp.

He hoisted the backpack once again onto his back and picked up Joy. "Today we make our way to the lookout."

"The lookout?"

Papa nodded then pointed to a mountain that stood proudly in the middle of the lake. *How did I not notice that?*

"Best view in the land. Can't wait for you to see it." He patted Joy and then turned to walk straight into the water.

Oh, God. Oh, God. He can't be serious. But He was. He had already made His way about twenty feet out in the water.

"Not a bad day, either. Water's pretty calm." His feet tapped the surface of the lake.

I tilted my head wondering if maybe, *just maybe*, the lake happened to be very, very shallow. I picked up a stone to test my theory and threw it out near Papa.

He watched it fall beneath the water, "Wow, it gets deep pretty quick."

"Not helping, Papa." I stared at the scene, the water lapping up on my toes on the beach.

"Sara, I really want you to see the lookout." Papa held Joy as she bobbed up and down in His arms, ready to run.

I wanted to see the lookout. It's just that stepping forward would require breaking away from the rules of the world, namely gravity at this moment, and I wasn't convinced she would let me go. What if she gripped me like a jealous love and held me underwater?

"Sara," His eyes steadied me. "I have overcome the world."

I stood there, shaking in my Chacos, thinking of how Peter was *the man* and I was a wimp. Papa sees impossible moments like new playground equipment, always excited to try them out. *Why was I so scared?*

I could hear Him like He was right beside me, soft and strong, "*Live with me.*"

My great desire. To live. To truly and abundantly live. And somehow I knew this was a part of it. Living meant knowing Him, experiencing Him. But I had to know Him in the impossible. I had to know His goodness and kindness were not limited by solid ground. His goodness would not change depending on my next step. His goodness would be there. Ready. Waiting. For me to rest on. I had to believe it.

So I closed my eyes, and began to sing.

I sang like a five-year-old making up her own Disney ballad. Clumsy and heartfelt words of who I knew Him to be. I stepped into the water and felt it cover my feet. Then it covered my ankles, and my calves. But my song would not desist. I sang like I was reminding the water who it belonged to. Long billowing notes of His kindness and beauty. My knees felt the water's cool embrace. Even if it consumed me, there was no other direction than to move towards Him. But that is precisely when gravity took its final bow and my shoe found sure footing on top of the lake.

I rose up on both feet still singing broken, wayward notes of deeply known love. He spoke softly in my ear, "Impossibility suits you, Beloved."

I opened my eyes just as Joy laid a wet one on my cheek and I giggled. "This. Is. Awesome."

Then we began to walk together. Papa and me on top of the water.

Joy fidgeting and fussing, anxious to be let down.

"Can Joy walk on water, Papa?"

"I've never seen her walk on water." He fought to hold her down.

Joy yipped and pushed, trying to break free from Papa's arms until she finally succeeded. Off she leapt, looking at me with that same sneaky grin I'd seen all those mornings she exited the hammock. Papa was right. Joy didn't walk on water. She ran. Like a bullet. And as she ran back and forth, the waves began to form. Papa shook his head smiling, "Oh, Joy."

I felt like I was standing in a boat on the rocking sea, minus the boat, leaning back and forth trying to keep my balance.

Papa offered me His hand, "Joy loves impossibility, and it's a good thing too."

"Why's that, Papa?" I grabbed hold tightly.

"Because when Joy plays in the water, you get to dance in the waves." He put His other hand behind my back and began to twirl me around the lake. We danced all the way across to the bottom of the lookout mountain.

Up until that point, I think that was the loudest I'd laughed in the Restlands.

You are faithful,
Oh Lord.
You are faithful,
Oh Lord.
You will take
my feet again
out of the sinking,
shifting sand
And you will place me to
stand
on the rock.

Only God can make a way
where there seems to be no way
Release Freedom, Jesus.
I have tasted and I've seen
the great feast that waits
for me
Praise Jesus, exalt
His name on high.

11

The Lookout

Joy shook the drops of her mad dash across the lake all over me. I looked back to our campsite from the previous night and marveled at the impossibility that had become our dance floor.

"Shall we?" Papa motioned to the trail.

Joy kicked the sand and shot up the path, her tail wagging like a motor. Papa and I followed, carefully placing our feet on the rocks and exposed tree roots. It was more of a climb than a hike today and with each step we rose higher above the Restlands. I felt like the land was watching me. The trees and streams, the waterfalls and wildlife, all watching like proud grandparents, gabbing to one another about how quickly I'd grown. I half expected the trees to pull out Polaroids to share and laugh about my days in the Restlands.

"What is it, Sara?" Papa asked.

"I feel like I'm being watched."

"You are." Papa whistled calling for Joy, she always liked to go before us. "Good girl, stay with us." He knelt down and scratched her ears.

"I am?"

"All of creation *is* watching you. Waiting."

"Waiting for what?" I knelt beside Him while Joy watched our conversation like a tennis match.

"For you to remember who you are." He smiled.

In this moment His smile was my sweet confidence. I stared at Him until a *knowing* resided in my heart, an assurance that remembering who I am was something I could not miss, something I could not fail. Staring at Papa was like remembering a childhood I had forgotten. I was sure, if I kept looking at Him, I would remember me. The real me. The free me.

The wild me.

I nodded and we rose for the final ascension up the trail, each step a declaration that I was here – walking with Him, making the Restlands my own.

The wind resounded like a standing ovation as we stepped out onto the lookout, and then quieted as if it awaited an acceptance speech. The lookout was larger than I expected, a round wooden deck with railing all around. In the middle stood a curious round pillar. Papa placed the hiking pack beside it and took my hand, leading me to the railing.

The Restlands. All of it, stretching in every direction like a quilt of landscapes, each patch telling its own story. I wanted to hear them all. I spotted the highway. I traced it trying to find my car, thinking back to that day when Papa's interruption had changed everything. I followed the distant line of the road as I walked around the lookout, expecting it to trail off into the horizon, pointing to all my dreams. But it didn't trail off. It followed me all the way around the lookout until I met Papa again and looked at Him with my mouth agape, "It's a circle?"

The smile lines around His eyes crinkled, "The highway?"

"Yes."

He leaned his elbows on the railing and looked out, "Round and around it goes."

"I was never going anywhere? Just driving around in a circle?" I felt swindled. *How could the road have been so cruel, so misleading? Had I been chasing after dreams that were never going to happen?*

"Do you remember what I said to you – at the beginning, Sara?"

"I wouldn't find what I was looking for on the road."

He turned to me and gently held my face, "The road is just a way to get around. Eventually everyone turns off the road. Because this is where dreams live. The Restlands. This is your home," He winked, "and your great adventure."

I placed my hands on His and closed my eyes. I saw myself back on the road and realized His love had hedged me in from the beginning. But I had never seen it this way. I had always seen life on the road a journey of second-guesses and probable missed opportunities. A place where you won or you lost. Where you were behind or you were ahead. Where hopefully I'd find Him in the end – and then at last rest. But it wasn't true. The road was really just 101 ways to discover His love. Just one more way of exploring the land. I felt Papa's forehead against mine as the sweetest words dropped deep inside me. *You will not miss out.*

And like a hot air balloon releasing each rope to take to the air, I felt a breaking inside. Things that had been anchored for years began to lose their grip and rise. Fear and rejection and confusion and every dark thing that had ever tried to give me a false sense of the land traveled up through my heart until I gripped Papa's hands like a woman in labor and screamed. Ferociously. Not in sadness or anger, but in acceptance. Acceptance of truth, like someone had given me a new mind and I was audibly releasing the old one. Papa never drew away. Even as I screamed, His words continued to flow deep. *You are loved. You are Mine. You are free.*

And suddenly, His words were louder inside me than the scream coming out of me, and I felt His tears wash my cheeks. I gasped for air and opened my eyes. I looked around, stunned, like I had somehow forgotten where I was, and then I looked in His eyes.

He smiled. "You're louder than you think," He whispered.

I shook my head and smiled back.

"Feeling better, Wild One?"

I nodded. *Wild One?* I *did* feel wild. I felt free. I felt alive. I felt like I could have wrestled the old me – and felt my shoulder ache in response.

"I have something for you." Papa turned and headed for the backpack.

I followed him and stood beside the pillar, which I noticed now was more of a barrel with leather pulled across the top. Papa stooped down and unzipped a pocket. He pulled out a pair of pristinely carved sticks, thicker on one end than the other. Along the sides were etches of places we'd seen along the trail. My fingers found the laughing bird and Joy running with her tongue out. If I looked even closer I could see words swirling amongst the pictures, the inside jokes and revelations of our time together.

"For you, Wild One." He turned towards the leather-covered barrel and beat it twice with His hands.

My eyes widened as I looked down at the whittled wood, "Drumsticks," I realized.

"Find your rhythm, Kiddo." He held His hands out towards the drum as an invitation.

The sun set to an uproar of celebration on the lookout. Papa had carved our story and placed it in my hands. This was my instrument. This was my worship. Our story   *this* is what satisfied.

Joy howled, Papa sang, and I found my rhythm, arms blazing at the top of the lookout.

It was the sound of one who is loved.

The sound of one who is free.

The sound of one who *lives* in the Restlands.

The sound of the
Restlands.
A song composed
of Joy and Papa
and me.
The whole world
is groaning,
waiting to hear it.
I will not keep it
waiting any longer.

The Wild One

The Epilogue

I sat against the drum watching the sunrise. The dewdrops on top of the railing sparkled, decorating a new day. I stroked the pages in my journal as I looked back through our journey and breathed deeply as my pencil tapped the next blank page.

Papa stood by the railing, like a ship's captain. I wondered what He thought of in the mornings. Did He consider the day ahead and all that must get done? Did He pause to look mindfully on the scenery? Or was He too remembering with fondness all the steps of our great trek? The Captain of Rest revealed no secrets, at least not in this moment.

My pencil awoke to the page. *Rest. Had I at last found it? Was rest something that could be found? Or was it something that had found me? Maybe rest was a land – hard to define and intended to explore. Perhaps rest was a journey of its own, made of moments that draw you deeper and deeper into calling the land 'home'. Maybe rest was Him. The One presiding over it now in His early morning mystery. 'Rest is a person' sounds as simplistic as 'Love is a person'. And yet there is nothing simple about such a definition. For who has ever known another fully – into the depths of their majesty and mystery. I may not ever come to the end of rest. But perhaps I had at last befriended it.*

Joy was sleeping in, curled up by my feet with her head gently laying on my leg. A rarity, for sure. I set my journal down and attempted to slip out from under her. She paid little attention, rolled over and began to snore. I gently picked up my drumsticks, momentarily held them to my heart, and then slipped them into my back pocket. I rose to join Papa.

He welcomed my hug. For a moment we stood quietly watching the Restlands awaken.

"What's out there?" I broke our silence.

"What do you mean?" Papa rubbed my arms, warming me in the morning chill.

"Beyond the road? Where does the Restlands end?"

"End?" He asked, as if unfamiliar with the word.

"Does it end, Papa?

His only response was a smile. One I'd seen a thousand times on this trip. One that seemed a simple reply, but I knew inherently it was not. Some questions were meant to be answered by more than words.

Joy stretched by my feet, finally joining the day. I picked her up. She admired the view briefly before falling asleep again in my arms.

"Oh, Joy," I laughed scratching behind her ears, "it's been quite a trip."

Papa patted Joy's head, "Such a good girl." He looked at me, the kindness on His face always refreshing, "this is where dreams live, Scribe."

I wondered if any dream could be as satisfying as this moment. But there was something about Papa reminding me about dreams that felt hopeful. I think He delighted in them and I think He wanted me to know it was okay to delight in them as well. I knew it was time. Time to find the dreams. But this time by foot. Maybe the journey would be what I was dreaming for all along.

Papa kissed my forehead and walked back towards the hiking pack. I looked across the land, planning my next route, "Are you ready for a great adventure, Joy?" I whispered. I turned around to join Papa.

But He wasn't there. I quickly studied the lookout and holding Joy tightly, ran to the where the trail descended. "Papa!" I cried out. But He was gone.

My journal was placed on top of the pack, ready for a new journey. Maybe I was ready too. I held Joy as I walked to the pack. She opened her eyes, squirmed and jumped down from my arms. She sniffed the perimeter of the railing until she found her way back to my foot and sat happily waiting for our departure. I picked up the journal and found a note tucked inside. His words were simple. They were all I needed to quickly place my journal away and pick up the pack. It seemed so much lighter than the first time.

"Are you ready, Joy?"

She wagged her tail and barked her allegiance. I smiled. A simple smile infused with anticipation. I felt deeply I had finally learned to smile like Papa. Now it was time to hike.

"Come on, Joy," I called, snapping my fingers as I began down the trail, "Sometimes what seems like the end, is only the beginning."

Welcome home, Scribe.

I am here.

Always.

And we have much more to discover.

- Papa

Join Papa, Scribe, and Joy

back on the trail soon

in

The Love Letters

About the Author

SARA RUST grew up overseas and returned to the United States to complete a film degree at Northwestern University. Following graduation, she moved to Cairo, Illinois where she was involved in community development as a missionary. In 2009, Sara moved to Redding, California to complete a Master's in Education and spend time teaching scores of action-packed third and fourth graders. Storytelling has weaved its way though every chapter, and has now, after much patience, won a more prominent place in her life.

Sara is an innovative storyteller of page, stage, and screen, journeying through life catching stories where they fly. Equipped with an overactive imagination, she loves writing stories that tell of the great Love that pursues us all.

Follow her journey at saramrust.com.

BASILEIA

"The land behind the silver door exploded with light and color. No one knew how big Basileia was or how many lifetimes it would take to find out. It was here the children would while away their days, free to do what they truly loved."

Basileia (Greek for *kingdom*) is the whimsical story of a village whose children spend their days in a hidden land. But when the children mysteriously begin to forget about the land behind the silver door, one brave girl must find a way to remember before Basileia is lost forever. Let wonder and dreams be awakened again as you too journey behind the silver door and discover what brings you life. Delight your heart with this timeless and inspiring storybook for young and old.

THE INVITATION

"Tears and tenderness at the very first pages. A lovely, intimate reflection on God's love for us. " **-Amazon Review**

"These whimsical short stories share what happens when different folks accept The Invitation. Among the recipients, a dancer, a gardener, a sports enthusiast, a writer, and more. Originally written as gifts to family and friends, this lovely book assures us that we are all beloved and unique. We are each meant for, and personally invited to, a Life fully engaged, exuberant, adventurous, and deeply satisfying. A pleasure to read and to share!." **-Amazon Review**

The Invitation is a collection of whimsical short stories that originated as gifts for friends and family, each a wild adventure and encounter with Papa. An invitation for one - is an invitation for all. Join the multitudes young and old who have found themselves in the pages - and discovered the great Love that pursues us all. Uncover what the pages hold for you. Journey into a world of wonder, where Love is chasing you down. For all have been invited. And Papa is patiently waiting.

KINGDOM TOOLS FOR TEACHING

"If you've been looking for how to create a godly revolution around you in the classroom, then you've found what you've been looking for. This book isn't a way to subversively have devotions or church in the classroom. In these pages you will find a template to show students freedom, love, joy, righteousness, hope and power."

Danny Silk, best-selling author of ***Keep Your Love On*** and ***Culture of Honor***

Kingdom Tools for Teaching brings both inspiration and practical tools to empower and activate you in bringing the Kingdom of God to ANY classroom. This is not a manual. This is the testimony of our breakthroughs and the tools that came from them. It is our heart to share these tools to inspire you to find your own and to adapt ours for your own classroom and school. We invite you to join us on a journey of stepping out of the mundane and into an adventure with Him that will shape students lives, the course of education and maybe even history itself.

THE BOOK MAKER

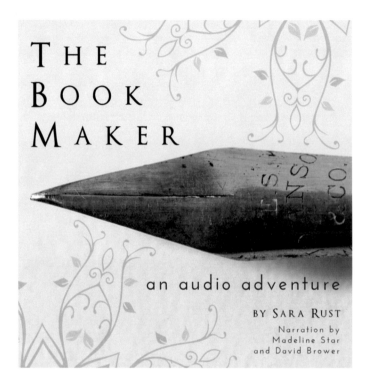

The Book Maker is a charming and mysterious audio short story, a new holiday classic for the whole family. This wintery tale will capture your heart as you too try to unravel the riddles of the library in the woods. Grab some hot cider and enter in. The door is surely open and the Book Maker is eagerly waiting, but remember not all is as it seems.

THE RESTLANDS

The Restlands returns as an audio adventure experience. Follow Scribe and Papa again, and relive the moving journey with music and sound as told by the author, herself. This rich tale will sweep you into the wilderness on a journey with God into the land of rest, where you just might hear things you've never heard before.